PEDRO
THE ANGEL OF OLVERA STREET

by
LEO POLITI

CHARLES SCRIBNER'S SONS
NEW YORK

ISBN 684-12628-1 (cloth)
ISBN 684-16003-X (paper)
13 15 17 19 RD/C 20 18 16 14 12
1 3 5 7 9 11 13 15 17 19 RD/P 20 18 16 14 12 10 8 6 4 2

*The Posada song is used
by courtesy of Padua Hill Theater*

to the children
of Olvera Street

ON OLVERA STREET in the heart of the big city of Los Angeles, Pedro and his grandfather played music and sang songs.

Pedro sang lovely Mexican songs, and when he sang to the music of his grandfather's violin crowds would gather around to listen, and often someone would say,

"Pedro sings like an angel."

Grandpa held Pedro's hand as they crossed the street from the old Mission Church to the Plaza, and then to Olvera Street.

"How things have changed since I was a little boy like you Pedro!" said Grandpa. "I can remember when this Mission Church, the Plaza and Olvera Street were the center of the Pueblo of Los Angeles. Then I saw the Pueblo grow all around — big and bigger. And look what a great city Los Angeles is now!"

"Olvera Street was so important then, and now how little and lost it is in the midst of such wide streets and tall buildings! But still it is beautiful is it not, Pedro?"

Yes, Pedro loved Olvera Street.

He loved the little street because it was just as it was in the days of the past, with the red-tiled pavement and the old adobe houses — where the birds fluttered around the fountain and fed among the footsteps.

He loved the humble little *puestos* (shops) lined along the center of the street and bulging with colorful wares.

He loved the smells of good Mexican foods:

    tacos

    tamales

    enchiladas

And music — there was always music everywhere.

And he loved Olvera Street because everyone was friendly and greeted him with a smile.

"Buenas dias, Pedro."

"Good morning, Pedro."

He liked to watch the many artisans

working at their interesting crafts.

PIRULI

Pedro had many friends with whom he played up and down the street.

They always came running to follow the organ-grinder with his amusing monkey.

They crowded around the puppet show and the little bullfight, where a trained dog took the part of the bull. Pedro liked this better than the real bullfight because this one was all in fun and no one ever got hurt.

They loved to suck *piruli*, a Mexican candy on a stick. Rosita sold it for only one penny.

But the best time of all the year for Olvera Street is Christmas time. Then the Street looks so gay, all decorated for the Christmas procession called La Posada.

This year Manuel was in charge of decorating the street. He took pride in making it look its best for the great event.

The children helped Manuel hang the large piñata, in the shape of a fantastic peacock, on a rope in the center of the street. The piñata was really an earthenware jar filled with candies and toys.

Pedro hoped that among the many toys in the piñata there would be a small music box, like the one he had seen in Tomaso's *puesto*. And how he wished to be the lucky one to get it when, on Christmas eve, the piñata was broken!

Manuel was also in charge of planning and directing the Posada.

The Posada is a procession which, like a Christmas play, tells the story of the journey of the Holy Mother Mary and Joseph to Bethlehem. It tells how they sought shelter (or posada) from the dark night and at last found refuge in a humble stable where the Christ Child was born.

First come the musicians, then come four people carrying the images of the Holy Family on a small wooden altar. Then in line, two by two, come the children, followed by the women and then the men.

This year Manuel thought of something that would make the procession even more beautiful. He had heard Pedro sing and he had heard people say, "Pedro sings like an angel." So he said:

"We must have an angel to lead La Posada."

He was so pleased with his idea that he hurried to Tomaso's puesto and asked him to make two little red wings for Pedro.

The Posada began on the sixteenth of December and journeyed through the street singing:

"We weary pilgrims
Come to your door
Shelter in your puesto
We beg, we implore."

But at every door they knocked the reply was," No! No! There is no shelter here. No posada."
And for nine nights, at the same hour each evening the Posada went through the street.

The people in the tall houses looked down on the Posada. Against the darkness of the night they could see the brightly lighted altar. The procession made a little trail of light, with the candles flickering joyfully.

And mounting to the sky, above the music and above the chorus, was Pedro's lovely voice. At the head of the procession he walked.

But until Christmas eve, no door would open to them.

And then on Christmas eve, the doors of a puesto were wide open.

"Enter Mary, Queen of Heaven."

"Enter Holy Joseph into this poor puesto!" And the Holy family entered to rest for the night. As they entered there was great joy and everyone sang:

s the Posada ended, the children came running to the place where the piñata hung.

"La piñata! La piñata!" they cried.

Before the game started the children got so impatient and noisy that Manuel had to raise his voice many times to keep order.

One by one in turn the children were blindfolded and with a stick tried to break the piñata.

"Dale, Juanita! Hit it, Juanita!"

"Dale! Dale! Dale! Hit it! Hit it! Hit it!" they cried.

Manuel held and pulled the rope from which the piñata hung and made it go up and down so it would be harder to hit and make the game more exciting.

There was much laughing and shouting. Whenever there was a close hit the excitement grew.

And as the music played they sang:

LA PIÑATA

Ti~ren con-fi-tes y ca-ne~lo~nes
Drop, oh Pi-ña-ta the love-ly small toys

pa los mucha-chos que son muy tra-gon--nes
to all the children so ea-ger-ly wait--ing

fin

2nd verse:

Anda muchacho, no te dilates - con los confetis y los cacahuates
Hit it Panchito! do not delay it - there will be candies and toys Christmas day

It was Pedro in his little red wings who landed a terrific hit and broke the piñata. Now the crowd grew more and more excited and the shouting children scrambled for the falling toys.

Pedro came out of the rush with his red wings a bit ruffled. But he was smiling and in his hands he held a small music box.

It was the music box he had wished for.

As it grew late the people began to go home, and the lights died down.

Soon the street became dark and deserted except for the bright light burning in the puesto over the little altar with the Holy Family.

Pedro was sleepy when he walked home that night. He leaned his head against grandpa and his wings drooped as if they, too, were tired.

"Buenas noches, Pedro."
"Good night, Pedro."

Now it was almost midnight, and Pedro was in his bed sound asleep and dreaming.

By his side the music box began to play softly. In the sky Pedro saw the bright star of Bethlehem shining down on Olvera Street. Then an angel with little red wings flew down from Heaven to sing a lovely song over the humble puesto where, once again, the Christ Child was born.